Iris and Walter
and the Birthday Party

Iris and Walter
and the Birthday Party

WRITTEN BY

Elissa Haden Guest

ILLUSTRATED BY

Christine Davenier

HARCOURT, INC.

ORLANDO   AUSTIN   NEW YORK
SAN DIEGO   TORONTO   LONDON

For Sheila, Baylie, Charlie, Rachel, and Jack.
And in loving memory of Jessie and Cork, two great book lovers—E. H. G.

Welcome to Anna Meiller—C. D.

Text copyright © 2006 by Elissa Haden Guest
Illustrations copyright © 2006 by Christine Davenier

www.HarcourtBooks.com

Library of Congress Cataloging-in-Publication Data
Guest, Elissa Haden.
Iris and Walter and the birthday party/written by Elissa Haden Guest;
illustrated by Christine Davenier.
p. cm.—(Iris and Walter; 10)
Summary: At Walter's birthday party his guests are supposed to go for horseback rides,
but his horse Rain has other plans on the day of the party.
[1. Parties—Fiction. 2. Birthdays—Fiction. 3. Horses—Fiction.]
I. Davenier, Christine, ill. II. Title. III. Series.
PZ7.G9375Iskq 2006
[E]—dc22 2005005013
ISBN-13: 978-0152-05015-3 ISBN-10: 0-15-205015-9

First edition

H G F E D C B A

Manufactured in China

Contents

1. The Invitation

One May day, a letter came for Iris.
It said:

Please come to
WALTER'S BIRTHDAY PARTY!
When: Saturday, May 11th
at two o'clock
Where: Walter's house
There will be cake and ice cream
and horse back riding.
Walter

"Oh boy!" said Iris.

"May I go to Walter's party?"

"Of course," said her mother.

"Absolutely," said her father.

"Mine, mine!" shouted Baby Rose.

"I have to tell Walter right away," said Iris.

And she hopped on her bike
and rode over to Walter's.

Walter was at the corral.

"Walter!" shouted Iris.

"I can come to your party!"

"Yippee!" yelled Walter.

"Goodness," said Iris, "Rain's belly is getting so big. When is she going to have a foal?"

"Oh, not for a while," said Walter.

Iris and Walter and Rain munched on carrots.

"I can't wait for your party," said Iris.

"Only five more days," said Walter.

"Everyone is going to like riding Rain,"
said Iris.
"It will be Rain's first birthday party!"
said Walter.
"We'll have to get her ready," said Iris.

"We'll give her a bath," said Walter.

"And comb her mane," said Iris.

"You'll be all dressed up for my party, Rain,"
said Walter.

And suddenly, Iris had an idea.

2. Iris's Surprise

That afternoon, Iris was very busy.

She drew.

She cut.

She sewed.

She glued.

And then she glued some more.

"What are you making, my girl?"
asked Grandpa.

"I'm making a present for Rain," said Iris.

16

"What is it going to be?" asked Iris's father.

"It's a surprise," said Iris.

"It is? Well, Rain is a lucky horse to be getting a surprise," said Iris's father.

After school on Friday,
Iris went over to Walter's.
"Tomorrow's my birthday party," sang Walter.
"So *you* have to take a bath, Rain," he said.
Iris and Walter washed Rain.
They dried her, and brushed her,
and combed her mane.

"I have a surprise for you, Rain," said Iris.
Iris gave Walter the present.
"Gosh! That's terrific. Thank you, Iris,"
said Walter. "Now you're all ready for the
party, Rain," he said.

That night, Walter was too excited
to eat his supper.

And when it was time for bed,
he could not settle down.

"I hope it doesn't rain tomorrow," he said.

"It's not going to rain," said Walter's mother.

"I hope everyone comes to my party,"
said Walter.

"They'll come, honey," said Walter's father.

Walter's mother and father tucked him in
and kissed him good night.
"Good night, sleep tight," said Walter's father.

But it was hard to settle down.
Walter kicked off his blankets and stared
at the moon in the big dark sky.
*I sure hope everyone has a good time at
my party,* Walter thought.
And, after a long while, he fell asleep.

3. Walter's Party

The next morning, the sky was
blue, blue, blue!
It was a wonderful day for a birthday party.
After breakfast, Walter raced outside.
"It's my birthday today, Rain!" he said.
Rain snorted.

"Time for your breakfast," said Walter.

Walter gave Rain her oats.

But Rain did not want to eat.

Rain lay down.

Rain got up.

Rain lay down.

Rain got up.

Rain could not settle down.

I think Rain is excited about my birthday, too,
thought Walter.

Walter sat outside and waited and waited
for his party to begin.
When is everyone coming? he thought.
And then, all of a sudden,
everyone was coming at once.

"Happy birthday, Walter," said Iris.

"Happy birthday, Walter,"
said Benny and Jenny and Lulu.

"Thank you," said Walter.

"Come on, everybody. Let's go ride Rain!"

Everybody tramped across the field
to the corral.
But Rain was not there.
"Rain must be in the barn,"
said Walter's mother.
"I'll go get her."

The children waited and waited.
At last, Walter's mother came outside.
"I'm afraid no one can ride Rain today,"
she said.

"Oh no!" said Walter. "Is Rain sick?"

"Not at all," said Walter's mother.

"I have a surprise for you.

Come with me, two at a time.

And you have to be very, *very* quiet," she said.

33

4. A Big Surprise

Walter and Iris tiptoed into the barn.

There was Rain, eating her oats.

Suddenly, Walter saw something move.

It was small.

It was brown.

It was lovely.

"Rain had her foal!" whispered Walter.
"Oh, it's beautiful," whispered Iris.

"She's a girl," said Walter's mother. "A filly."

"She's cute," whispered Benny.

"Horsey, horsey!" shouted Baby Rose.

"And when Rain is feeling ready,
you can all come back and ride her,"
said Walter's mother.

"Now, who's ready for cake?" she asked.

When the candles were lit,
everyone sang "Happy Birthday"
to Walter. Iris sang the loudest of all.
And Walter felt shy,
and a little embarrassed,
but very loved.

After the party, Iris and Walter
went to the barn to see Rain's foal.
"What are you going to name her?" asked Iris.

"I don't know," said Walter.

"What about Star?" asked Iris.

"Hmm," said Walter.

"What about Ginger?" asked Iris.

"Hmm," said Walter.

Walter thought and thought.

"I know!" he said.

"I'll name her Surprise," he said.

"Hello, little Surprise," said Iris.

"I wonder if she knows it's her birthday, too," said Walter.

"We should sing 'Happy Birthday' to her," said Iris.

And that is just what they did.

RICHMOND HTS

The illustrations in this book were created in pen-and-ink on keacolor paper.
The display type was set in Elroy.
The text type was set in Fairfield Medium.
Color separations by Colourscan Co. Pte. Ltd., Singapore
Manufactured by South China Printing Company, Ltd., China
This book was printed on totally chlorine-free Stora Enso Matte paper.
Production supervision by Ginger Boyer
Designed by Lauren Rille